GAULISH VILLAGE

COMPENDIUM

LAUDANUM

AQUARIUM

TOTORUM

ARMORICA

LUTETIA

SPQR

GAUL
(ROMAN CONQUEST)
50 BC

CELTICA

AQUITANIA

PROVINCIA

THE YEAR IS 50 BC. GAUL IS ENTIRELY OCCUPIED BY THE
ROMANS. WELL, NOT ENTIRELY ... ONE SMALL VILLAGE OF
INDOMITABLE GAULS STILL HOLDS OUT AGAINST THE INVADERS.
AND LIFE IS NOT EASY FOR THE ROMAN LEGIONARIES WHO
GARRISON THE FORTIFIED CAMPS OF TOTORUM, AQUARIUM,
LAUDANUM AND COMPENDIUM ...

ASTERIX, THE HERO OF THESE ADVENTURES. A SHREWD, CUNNING LITTLE WARRIOR, ALL PERILOUS MISSIONS ARE IMMEDIATELY ENTRUSTED TO HIM. ASTERIX GETS HIS SUPERHUMAN STRENGTH FROM THE MAGIC POTION BREWED BY THE DRUID GETAFIX . . .

OBELIX, ASTERIX'S INSEPARABLE FRIEND. A MENHIR DELIVERY MAN BY TRADE, ADDICTED TO WILD BOAR. OBELIX IS ALWAYS READY TO DROP EVERYTHING AND GO OFF ON A NEW ADVENTURE WITH ASTERIX – SO LONG AS THERE'S WILD BOAR TO EAT, AND PLENTY OF FIGHTING. HIS CONSTANT COMPANION IS DOGMATIX, THE ONLY KNOWN CANINE ECOLOGIST, WHO HOWLS WITH DESPAIR WHEN A TREE IS CUT DOWN.

GETAFIX, THE VENERABLE VILLAGE DRUID, GATHERS MISTLETOE AND BREWS MAGIC POTIONS. HIS SPECIALITY IS THE POTION WHICH GIVES THE DRINKER SUPERHUMAN STRENGTH. BUT GETAFIX ALSO HAS OTHER RECIPES UP HIS SLEEVE . . .

CACOFONIX, THE BARD. OPINION IS DIVIDED AS TO HIS MUSICAL GIFTS. CACOFONIX THINKS HE'S A GENIUS. EVERY-ONE ELSE THINKS HE'S UNSPEAKABLE. BUT SO LONG AS HE DOESN'T SPEAK, LET ALONE SING, EVERYBODY LIKES HIM . . .

FINALLY, VITALSTATISTIX, THE CHIEF OF THE TRIBE. MAJESTIC, BRAVE AND HOT-TEMPERED, THE OLD WARRIOR IS RESPECTED BY HIS MEN AND FEARED BY HIS ENEMIES. VITALSTATISTIX HIMSELF HAS ONLY ONE FEAR, HE IS AFRAID THE SKY MAY FALL ON HIS HEAD TOMORROW. BUT AS HE ALWAYS SAYS, TOMORROW NEVER COMES.

THE FOREST OF THE CARNUTES IS SWARMING WITH DRUIDS IN MERRY MOOD, ALL DELIGHTED TO SEE EACH OTHER AGAIN...

EVERY OAK TREE IS FULL OF DRUIDS HARD AT WORK CUTTING MISTLETOE WITH THEIR SICKLES...

SNIP!

SNIP!

SWISH!

OOOOUCH! THAT'S MY FINGER!

THEY TALK SHOP, THEY DISCUSS SPELLS...

YES, MY DEAR FELLOW, I PICKED UP THIS SICKLE IN A LITTLE SHOP IN DARIORIGUM! LOOK, IT'S GOT A SAFETY-CATCH.

CLACLACLAC

SO THEN, OLD MAN, HEY PRESTO! I TURNED HIM INTO A MENHIR!

THEY EVEN INDULGE IN JOKES AND PUNS... IN SHORT, THEY ARE HAVING A GOOD TIME

THIS FOOD'S A BIT SICKLE-Y!

PASS ME THE CELT!

IT MUST BE HIS GAUL-BLADDER!

MENHIR A TRUE WORD IS SPOKEN IN JEST!

THEN, AFTER THE GREAT BANQUET...

SILENCE, BROTHERS, SILENCE!

CLANG!

CLANG!

CLANG!

BROTHER DRUIDS, THE TIME HAS COME FOR US TO BEGIN OUR GREAT CONTEST TO EVALUATE NEW METHODS AND ELECT THE DRUID OF THE YEAR...

AND WHILE THE DRUIDS PREPARE THEIR MAGIC POTIONS...

...GREEDY EYES ARE WATCHING THEM...

Now comes the interesting part!

⑥

10

THINGS ARE GETTING COMPLICATED. NOT ONLY HAVE WE LOST TIME, BUT THE ROMANS WILL BE AFTER US NOW!

AND IN A NEARBY ROMAN CAMP, IN THE TENT OF GENERAL CANTANKERUS...

BY JUPITER! IT SEEMS INCREDIBLE! BARBARIANS WANDERING ABOUT ON ROMAN TERRITORY AND GETTING AWAY WITH IT! IF JULIUS CAESAR HEARS OF THIS, WE'LL ALL BE SERVED UP IN THE CIRCUS AS THE LIONS' DINNER!

AVE, GENERAL! THE PATROL IS BACK!

SEND THE LEADER IN!

AVE, GENERAL! WE FOUND THE HORDE OF BARBARIANS, BUT WE WERE DEFEATED.

TELL ME WHAT THIS HORDE WAS LIKE.

THERE WAS A FAT ONE AND A LITTLE ONE!

I'LL DRAW YOU A PICTURE...

GET COPIES OF THIS PICTURE MADE AND HAVE THEM SENT TO EVERY CAMP IN THE AREA!

WE'VE GOT TO LAY HANDS ON THOSE TWO GOTHS!

HANDS WILL BE LAID ON THEM ALL RIGHT, AND IT WON'T TAKE LONG, I CAN PROMISE YOU THAT!

RUNNERS SET OFF IN ALL DIRECTIONS...

...AND SOON AFTERWARDS

SOMEONE'S COMING!

LET'S CLIMB THIS TREE!

12

16

AS SOON AS THE ROMANS KNOW THAT THE GOTHS THEY ARE LOOKING FOR ARE DISGUISED AS ROMANS, THERE IS COMPLETE CHAOS... THE ROMANS GO ABOUT CAPTURING ONE ANOTHER...

I'M TAKING YOU IN, GOTH!

YOU OFF YOUR HEAD OR SOMETHING?

I'M A ROMAN! I'M A ROMAN! I'M A ROMAN!

GOT YOU, YOU BARBARIAN!

THE UNHAPPY GENERAL CANTANKERUS IS NEARLY OUT OF HIS MIND...

THEY'RE ALL QUITE THICK, AND I'M THEIR LEADER! (SOB! SOB!)

BUT SOME PEOPLE ARE MAKING THE MOST OF THE SITUATION. FOR INSTANCE, ASTERIX AND OBELIX, WHO HAVE PUT THEIR OWN CLOTHES ON AGAIN...

...AND THE GOTHS, THE ROOT OF ALL THE TROUBLE, WHO ARE PROCEEDING UNEVENTFULLY TOWARDS THEIR OWN COUNTRY OF GERMANIA.

Watch out! The frontier's ahead. We've got to cross it!

A HEAVY RESPONSIBILITY WEIGHS ON THOSE WHO GUARD THE FRONTIER AGAINST FOREIGN INVADERS...

GAUL
ROMAN EMPIRE

Germania

Hey!

MMMM?

BONG!

Victory is ours! We'll be given a hero's welcome by our own people!

Anything to declare?

18

24

WATCH OUT! SOMEONE'S COMING.

Who are you?

I DON'T UNDERSTAND GOTHIC, BUT I THINK HE'S ASKING WHO WE ARE...

AVE, BY JUPITER! I'M LEGIONARY OBELUS AND MY FRIEND IS LEGIONARY ASTERUS!

!

CHCHCHCHCHCHCHCH!

If I'm not much mistaken, these are Romans coming to invade us. Let's get them!

BOUM! PAFF! BIMM!

LET'S GO AND HIDE IN THE UNDERGROWTH, OBELIX. THERE ARE ONE OR TWO THINGS I MUST EXPLAIN...

WE DON'T HAVE TO PRETEND TO BE ROMANS ANY MORE, OBELIX. WE'D BE BETTER OFF DISGUISED AS GOTHS...

WHY?

ARE YOU READY, OBELIX? HERE'S YOUR SIZE COMING!

Hey!

ONE HOUR LATER...

AT LAST! I THOUGHT THIS ONE WAS NEVER GOING TO TURN UP!

21

OUCH!

LET'S PUT THE GOTHIC HELMETS OVER OUR GAULISH ONES. THAT'LL HELP US LOOK MORE CONVINCING!

WHAM!

BIFF!

RIGHT!

JUST REMEMBER, WE DON'T KNOW THEIR LANGUAGE, SO ON NO ACCOUNT SPEAK TO ANY GOTHS!

WE CAN BASH THEM THOUGH, CAN'T WE?!!

MEANWHILE...

O Metric, Rhetoric the interpreter is here!

Show him in!

If this druid refuses my demands, I shall be very angry, Rhetoric. I shall have the druid killed, and you along with him. Understand?

R...yes!

Ask him if he's prepared to use his magic powers in our cause...

ARE YOU PREPARED TO USE YOUR MAGIC POWERS IN OUR CAUSE?

NEVER!

Perhaps...

TELL HIM TO SAY YES OR NO!

YES OR NO?

NO!

YES!

Excellent! When will he show us his magic?

In a week's time, at the full moon.

PHEW! THAT GIVES ME A BREATHING SPACE!

22

28

ASTERIX AND OBELIX ARE NOT THE ONLY ONES WITH ESCAPE IN MIND FOR IN ANOTHER PART OF THE TOWN...

I'LL GO TO GAUL. WITH MY KNOWLEDGE OF MODERN LANGUAGES I'LL BE ABLE TO GET A JOB THERE...

Halt! Who goes there?

THE PATROL!

Well, if it isn't Rhetoric the interpreter! And where might you be off to at this time of night?

Well, I... er... the fact is... well, it was like this, you see...

No, I don't! It's the guardroom for you! You can explain yourself tomorrow!

No, no! You're making a big mistake! I've got friends in high places!!!

I'M DONE FOR! THE CHIEF WILL NEVER FORGIVE ME FOR DECEIVING HIM ABOUT WHAT THAT PIG-HEADED DRUID SAID...

MEANWHILE...

GOT IT? NO FIGHTING, AND NO TALKING TO ANY GOTHS.

RIGHT!

!

EEEK! THAT'S TORN IT!

Hullo, hullo, hullo! Who have we here? You're for the guardroom too!

㉕

29

30

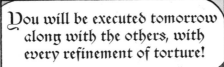

34

35

*THIS GAME, QUINQUIREMES AND GALLEYS IS STILL PLAYED DURING LESSONS TODAY, THOUGH THE PLAYERS IF DISCOVERED, MAY FIND THEMSELVES IN DIRE STRAITS.

Now, everyone listen to me! I've got some of the Gaulish druid's magic powers! I'm your new chief, Rhetoric I!

That's the stuff! Down with Metric!

Hurrah! Long live Rhetoric I!

PLATCH!

CLAP CLAP CLAP!

Just a minute! I'm the chief around here!

Throw this poor fish into the dungeons! It's time you were going, Metric.

SOON AFTERWARDS, IN THE PALACE...

COME ALONG IN, FRIENDS, COME ALONG IN. I WAS JUST PLANNING THE PROGRAMME FOR METRIC'S TORTURE TOMORROW.

What were we saying?

Well, and then we could put him in a double saucepan and stir over a slow flame...

SORRY TO INTERRUPT YOU, RHETORIC, BUT WE HAVE A FAVOUR TO ASK YOU...

YES? ANYTHING YOU LIKE, MY DEAR ASTERIX!

WE WANT TO VISIT METRIC IN HIS DUNGEON, TO CROW OVER HIM...

AN EXCELLENT IDEA! OFF YOU GO! HAVE A NICE TIME!

IT'S STILL WORKING!

When these Gauls have served their purpose I'll have to get rid of them...

I've got something special for them: a pressure cooker. It can cook a person in a couple of minutes, and it whistles when he's done!

Hee, hee! You can't stop progress!

36

ASTERIX, GETAFIX AND OBELIX MAKE THEIR WAY BACK TO THE DUNGEON FOR A WORD WITH METRIC...

Metric, would you like to get your revenge on Rhetoric and return to power?

?

HE SAYS YES!

I GOT THE GENERAL IDEA!

Have a swig of this magic potion... then you'll be as strong as Rhetoric. The way you use your strength is up to you...

!

GLUG! GLUG!

CLINNNK!

HE'S GOT A FREE HAND NOW!

CRAAAASH!

Here we go again! They ought to replace that door with a curtain!

Raise the alarm! The prisoner's escaping!!!

So what?

POC!

HE'S GOT A FREE HAND! HA! HA! HA! THAT'S A GOOD ONE, THAT IS! I'VE ONLY JUST GOT IT. HO! HO! HO!

37

41

42

ANOTHER CANDIDATE!

Drink this!

GLUG! GLUG!

AND OUR THREE GAULS CARRY ON WITH THEIR CAMPAIGN TO DISTURB THE PEACE...

Drink this!

GLUG! GLUG!

GLUG! GLUG!

Drink this!

GLUG! GLUG!

Drink this!

GLUG! GLUG!

Drink this!

GLUG! GLUG!

Drink this!

...WHILE EVERY ONE OF THEIR PATIENTS, INVINCIBLY STRONG AND SPURRED ON BY THE REMARKS OF OUR FRIENDS, SETS OUT TO RECRUIT AN ARMY...

TCHOC!

And that makes 250 — a company.

FIGHTING STARTS BETWEEN THE DIFFERENT FACTIONS...

Rhetoric for chief!

Metric for chief!

Up with Electric!

BING!

PAF!

Euphoric for chief!

THE GOURD OF POTION IS EMPTY...

BUT WHAT WILL HAPPEN WHEN THE GOTHS FIND THE EFFECTS OF THE POTION WEARING OFF?

NOTHING. THEY'LL ALL BE IN THE SAME BOAT. BEING MORE OR LESS EQUAL, THEY'LL GO ON FIGHTING EACH OTHER FOR CENTURIES... AND THEY WON'T STOP TO THINK ABOUT INVADING THEIR NEIGHBOURS.

WELL, NOW THAT OUR PEACE-MAKING MISSION IS ACCOMPLISHED, ALL WE HAVE TO DO IS GO HOME TO GAUL!

OOH, YES! I CAN'T WAIT TO TASTE WILD BOAR THE WAY MOTHER MADE IT!

40

Metric

Rhetoric

THE ASTERIXIAN WARS

A Tangled Web...

The ruse employed by Asterix, Getafix and Obelix succeeded beyond their wildest dreams. After drinking the druid's magic potion, the Goths fought each other tooth and nail. Here is a brief summary to help you follow the history of these famous wars.

The favourite and devastating weapon of the combatants.

Diagram indicating the course of events.

The first victory is won outright by Rhetoric, who, having surprised Metric by an outflanking movement, lets him have it – bonk! – and inflicts a crushing defeat on him. This defeat, however, is only temporary...

Rhetoric has no time to celebrate his victory, for, having completed his outflanking movement, he is taken in the rear by his own ally, Lyric. Lyric instantly proclaims himself supreme chief of all the Goths, much to the amusement of the other chiefs...

Who turn out to be right, for Lyric's brother-in-law Satiric lays an ambush for him, pretending to invite him to a family reunion, and Lyric falls into the trap. It was upon this occasion that the proposition that blood is thicker than water was first put to the test...

Rhetoric goes after Lyric, with the avowed intention of "bashing him up" (archaic), but his rearguard is surprised by Metric's vanguard. Bonk! This manoeuvre is known as the Metric System.

General Electric manages to surprise Euphoric meditating on the conduct of his next few campaigns. Euphoric's morale is distinctly lowered, but he has the last word, with his famous remark, "I'll short-circuit him yet".

While Electric proclaims himself supreme chief of the Goths, to the amusement of all and sundry, it is the turn of Metric's rearguard to be surprised by Rhetoric's vanguard. Bonk! "This is bad for my system," is the comment of the exasperated Metric.

In fact, it is so bad for his system that he allows himself to be surprised by Euphoric. The battle is short and sharp. Euphoric, a wily politician, instantly proclaims himself supreme chief of the Goths. The other supreme chiefs are in fits...

Euphoric, much annoyed, sets up camp and decides to sulk. He is surprised by Eccentric, who in his turn is attacked by Lyric, subsequently to be defeated by Electric. Electric is destined to be betrayed by Satiric, who will be beaten by Rhetoric.

Going round a corner, Rhetoric's vanguard bumps into Metric's vanguard. Bonk! Bonk! This battle is famous in the Asterixian wars as the "Battle of the Two Losers". And so the war goes on...

MEANWHILE, OUR THREE FRIENDS ARE APPROACHING THE FRONTIER OF GAUL, WITH THEIR MINDS AT REST...

41